SUBMARINER TALES

TRUTH OR FICTION YOU DECIDE

SUBMARINER TALES

TRUTH OR FICTION YOU DECIDE

DEAN S. LEWIS

AuthorHouse™ LLC
1663 Liberty Drive
Bloomington, IN 47403
www.authorhouse.com
Phone: 1-800-839-8640

Published by AuthorHouse 07/11/2013

ISBN: 978-1-4817-6108-6 (sc)
ISBN: 978-1-4817-6107-9 (e)

Library of Congress Control Number: 2013910408

This book is printed on acid-free paper.

Contents

Contents

Dedication

This book is dedicated to **GOD** who enabled the **Submariners** and their submarines to keep their countries safe at a time when **World War III** looked like it would be a nuclear holocaust during the **Cold War.**

Foreword

Submarines have always been a fascinating Naval experience in which men have served their various countries during wars of various lengths. The "Cold War" was no exception and went from 1946 to 1991.

These are tales to educate and inform you of the adventures of these extreme fighting machines, as well as the men and abilities of both.

Interestingly, there is no way of knowing if these stories are true or not as they are part of the Secret Service.

This is what makes this an interesting book in which YOU get to decide, and should you choose, then you may fill in your decisions of truth or fiction at the back of this book.

I am thrilled to have been asked to do this task to enlighten you and help the Museum of Naval History continue to educate you on the Secret Service and other naval services.

THE LIFE OF A SUBMARINER

Top Secret Regiment of the Navy once dressed like dockworkers

When it came to submarines, Dean Lewis knew all too well what the life of a submariner was like. Dean, who was known as Leading Seamen Roth when he served in the Royal Canadian Navy (he was legally adopted by his stepfather), served on all three submarines during the Cold War—the Onondaga, the Okanagan and the Ojibwa, now located in Port Burwell.

Hailing from Woodstock, Dean enlisted at Centennial Hall in London at age 17. He was ready to serve his country and protect its citizens. His love of the water aided his decision to join the Navy. Looking back on his early years, he recalled, "If you would find me anywhere in my childhood, it was always near water or the pool or the beach. My birthfather and grandfather were both part of the Air Force and they were somewhat disappointed that I joined the Navy, but they were glad I went into the military."

As a sonar operator, Dean's job included being the lookout on the surface and a helmsman under the water. As a helmsman he was responsible for steering and maintaining the depth of the ship. Inside the submarine, up to seventy people could be stationed. Today Dean refers to that group of seventy as a large family—one that could kill you if someone wasn't paying attention to his job.

How did those seventy people fit into one submarine? That's something Dean says you'll have to tour the sub to find out. He explains "When people ask me what it was like, I often ask them a question—Let's say you have a 12 by 15 foot room. Now, invite ten of your best friends over for the weekend and don't leave the room. If you can come out of that after the weekend with no anxieties, you have a good idea what it was like."

The submarines were used during the Cold War; a war Dean says was about nuclear domination between the United States and Russia. It ended with the fall of communism and the dissolution of the USSR in 1991. Dean likens it to playing cat and mouse, "We're a killer submarine. Our job is to remove a nuclear submarine. If you can't hear us, you can't see us, then you can't find us and we have the upper hand. That was basically our job and when we weren't on that part of the Cold War our job included training our ships and other submarines to be able to find us."

Dean served with the Navy from 1982 to 1988 and left after six and a half years to be with his family.

Submariners normally get between seven months to one year to learn the entire workings of the sub, and are then issued their Dolphins, which is akin to a pilot getting his wings. This signifies you are the elite of the elite.

Having served on Ojibwa, Dean thinks it's a huge advantage for many people in the country to have the sub in Port Burwell. Not only will it help people understand who submariners are, but it will also help explain what the Cold War was about. This part of the Navy was top secret. "Some families didn't even know you were part of the submarines," he says. When his wife asked how his day was, he would only answer that it was fine. Submariners eschewed typical military uniforms and instead dressed in jeans and t-shirts when they boarded in order to blend in with dockworkers so that no one knew they were on the submarines.

"I think generally people need to know that when we left a port in Halifax, we never knew if we were coming back because WWIII was imminent at that point in time. As we now know, it didn't happen, but it still looks like WWIII could be down the road." He calls Ojibwa the most unique artifact in Ontario, one that is going to create an incredible amount of structure for the area.

Edited from original written by Melissa Schneider from the St. Thomas/Elgin Weekly News dated February 28, 2013.

THE TALES

The First Submarine and Submariner Known to Man

This is perhaps the most unusual definition of a submarine but the truth of this submarine comes from our Creator GOD and is found in the Bible.

The story comes from Jonah chapter 1 verse 17, "And the LORD appointed a great fish to swallow Jonah, and Jonah was in the stomach of the fish three days and three nights." Jonah prayed to GOD from the stomach of the fish *(which you can look up yourself)*. After the prayer we are at Jonah chapter 2 verse 10 which says "Then the LORD commanded the fish, and it vomited Jonah up onto dry land."

This story starts with GOD as commander of all, who had asked Jonah, *(approximately 762 B.C.)*, to go five hundred miles east to Nineveh to preach to the city's wicked residents. *(population 120,000)* Jonah decides he will disobey GOD and run from his destiny and gets on a ship that is heading two thousand miles west to Tarshish.

The Captain is GOD, the fish is the submarine, and Jonah is the first submariner. The journey was a short three days and nights somewhere in the Mediterranean Sea between Joppa *(the modern city of Jaffa which is a suburb of Tel Aviv, Israel)* towards Tarshish *(which is now Spain)* and Nineveh. Nineveh was the capital city of the mighty Assyrian Empire, which was destroyed about 150 years after this story in 612 B.C.

As a submariner myself I can hardly imagine what Jonah was going through. I am sure it felt like a lifetime being inside this fish and less comfortable and spacious than submarines of today that are made by man.

Perhaps we could demonstrate this like a three day bath with no food. Imagine some seaweed or smaller fish floating by us—would we even know what it was floating by us or would we want to know?

I wonder what the smell of the innards would be like for the three days and nights *(not a long weekend that I would enjoy)* with a very unpleasant aroma, making diesel fumes seem harmless. There would be no light or idea where we were headed and if that isn't enough—picture having salt water all over you at the same time. Now the question we all want to ask, but do not really want to know the answer—Where do you go to the washroom?

The final way out is by Jonah being vomited up and onto dry land. Not a smooth sailing into port, tying up at harbor stations and walking off of submarine to step back on land after a long journey at sea.

I am thankful that my time aboard was a 'walk in the park' in comparison to what Jonah our first submariner went through despite never knowing if we would return home during the "Cold War."

The First Submarine and Submariner Known to Man

Canadian Submarine in the Falklands

This story starts out with a Canadian Submarine doing normal patrol in the North Atlantic in April of 1982.

The communications were going wild. Reports of Argentina taking control of the Falkland Islands on April 2, 1982 had occurred. This was the largest naval contingency since World War II which was confirmed by Maritime Command on April 3, 1982 *(approximately 110 ships)*. Maritime Command then let England send communications to Canadian O boat *(Oberon Class submarine)* to head towards South Atlantic to aide the British in any way.

Vice Admiral Herbert was in charge of all submarine activity and sent areas of operation by crypto gear *(a specially coded message that could only be deciphered by this unique equipment)*. On April 5 the order came across the crypto gear to head due south on a course headed directly towards the Falklands and maintain a barrier for the British Fleet in the unfortunate case that their Submarines were damaged or destroyed. May 4, 1982—received message to head north to Ascension Island at midnight to be refueled and restocked with food and return to barrier location until further notice.

On May 22, the radioman received another crypto message informing Canadian Submarine to break barrier and head for the Falklands undetected. Support due to HMS (*Her Majesty's Ship*) Onyx taking bow damage, making her attack sonar inoperable, *(unconfirmed cause of damage)* This often meant they were landing SBS *(Special Boat Service)* and were engaged or hit something coming out from close to shore.

The Canadian Submarine took HMS Onyx's position while she headed to Ascension Island for repairs. May 27, 1982—Canadian O boat was in place of the coast of South Georgia to assist SBS riders in and out of the island. Unfortunately two did not return for the pickup and were reported MIA. *(Missing In Action)* It would be reported years later that they were killed by their counterparts—the SAS *(Special Air Service)*.

The Argentine forces surrendered 74 days after taking the Falklands on June 14, 1982 and the Canadian Submarine returned to Halifax on June 28th with no knowledge reported of where they were or what they did.

Looking forward to your thoughts on this tale being true or false and any comments you may wish to make by sending in the form at the back of the book.

Canadian Submarine in the Falklands

No More Volunteers for Silent Service

The volunteer submariner program ended in 1986. This decision caused many of the best submariners to leave due to safety onboard. It is based on issues unknown to many except those making this terrible determination.

One would think that not having enough submariners who wanted to do their job and protect their country would not be the reason for sending personnel, *(which did not want to be on submarines)*, into duty in the silent service. Being a submariner at this time only caused grief and headaches for qualified submariners due to personnel not wanting to serve in this naval establishment.

It takes from seven months to a year to be qualified as a submariner. This means you have earned your "Dolphins" in which you have hands-on knowledge of every system and position on board the submarine. Therefore you had to do this on your own time at sea if you were on the two-watch system. That meant you did your trade for six hours then you had six hours off. During that "off time" you would have to eat, do cleaning stations and most likely an exercise for safety aboard, leaving virtually no time to rest. You then hoped in your next 6 hours off you would get a couple hours of sleep. The other watch system was four hours on your trade followed by eight hours off giving you more time for rest and to qualify as a submariner.

The problem arose when the military chose to cancel volunteers and send trades as needed to submarines, causing nightmares and issues to the qualified submariner. The qualified submariner known as a "Sea Daddy" now attempted to train the "Sea Puppy" assigned to him. You can imagine the headache, as one mistake from an unqualified or qualified submariner could kill all 70 aboard. If a person didn't want to be onboard or they don't want to do their training, they would often intentionally screw up. This forced the qualified submariner to verify everything the unqualified submariner did to ensure the safety of all aboard.

Due to this extra frustration, the onboard submariners could no longer trust that the other submariners had their back to ensure that everything would remain safe. A situation like this causes turmoil on a regular basis at sea.

It has been said that qualified submariners were the "Elite" and were the most highly trained. They were also known as "Unique" possibly "Crazy" and perhaps not "All There."

My thought is they were the "Best of the Best" and that ensured that no matter the issues they faced, they adapted as necessary to maintain the safety of their country and its citizens. I wonder what your thoughts are and if you believe this to be true or false? Again you get to decide and feel free to comment should you fill in the back page of this book.

No More Volunteers for Silent Service

Submariners Ashore

Canadian submarine alongside in Savannah, Georgia sometime during the Cold War after a 28 day patrol at sea.

Submariners were put up in hotels when in ports and given an allowance for *food (unsure of exact amount so it has not been stated, but it covered breakfast, lunch, and dinner)*. Four Submariners *(two stokers and two sonar men)* decided to go to one of the local bars to enjoy some relaxation and hopefully have a game or two of pool. Oh yes, and have some drinks, which was always the way to cope in those days.

After a couple of drinks one of the sonar men passed through the pool hall area to go to the washroom. On his way back to his three submariner friends the patrons in the pool area decided they wanted his money and pulled a knife on him. He called for his buddies *(he was outnumbered)* and kicked the knife out of the assailant's hand while his buddies helped diffuse the situation. There were two gentlemen at the bar drinking that witnessed the whole thing. *(It was discovered later that day that they were undercover detectives)*

Things settled down and three of the submariners decided it best to leave and find a better drinking establishment. Unfortunately the other sonar man thought it would be better to fight the pool patrons to let them know that their actions were unacceptable. The three submariners started to escort the sonar man out the door when he again decided he was going in to clean out the bar. Our first sonar man reacted quickly at the outside entry to the bar grabbing the second sonar man, who tried to spin out of the hold, thus crashing through the neighboring store front window. The first sonar man quickly acted to pull the second sonar man out of the window area as a shower of glass from above came down like a guillotine.

The next thing heard were gun shots and our first sonar man dropped the second sonar man back into the window front, while all three submariners ran from the scene. One of the stokers ran three blocks and hid under a parked car. The second stoker ran directly in the opposite direction and found another bar to walk into and sat down and enjoyed a drink, while our first sonar man ran 12 blocks to the hotel he was staying at. He knocked on doors for someone to let him in, *(which no one did),* while the police swarmed the area. One police car spotted our sonar man and called for backup cars to surround the hotel.

The first sonar man was now on the top floor with nowhere to go when a 300 pound local policeman yelled "Stop, hit the ground or I'll shoot." Naturally the sonar man went to his knees and to his surprise had the policeman's gun barrel shoved against his head. The female officer in charge had our sonar man handcuffed and she and her partner started to escort him to the Savannah Police Station downtown. Our submariner tried to explain that it was his buddy whom he saved from a bar fight and whom would have been killed by the window coming down like a guillotine.

As the two officers and our first sonar man were walking up the stairs to the station, the radio report came in from on site. The call verified that our submariners were not trying to mug the submariner in the window but were indeed saving his life. The first submariner was then escorted back to the submarine by the police officers and told to take care of the damages before leaving.

Back at the hotel the next day, our first submariner called the store that had the broken window to repair it and to his surprise it was already being done. The owner asked who wanted to know and the submariner quickly answered with the untrue name of "John Fairbourne." He told the owner to let him know if there were any problems.

This is certainly an interesting tale and I wonder what you think? Is it true or false?

Submariners Ashore

Fast Cruise

This is the story of an exercise that was scheduled for about a week in which you trained every day without knowledge of what exercise would be next.

It started with Harbor Stations alongside Halifax where you left port and headed to sea. Once you were about 10 miles off the coast, you "opened up for dive" where submariners used a checklist to confirm that all valves were in the proper position for diving. This was then verified by an officer and sent to the control room. When reports were sent from each compartment—forward torpedo room, accommodation space, engine room, motor room and the after torpedo room *(later known as the after accommodation space)* and the control room was opened up for a dive, then it was safe to dive submarine.

The Captain told the helmsman *(operator of one-man control which enabled both steering and depth of submarine)* "Dive to 85 feet and level off at 60 feet." *(periscope depth)* Other submariners checked hatches in each compartment and reported back "no leaks" or "worse leak in accommodation space hatch." In the event of a leak, the Captain ordered helmsman to surface and try to repair the leak at sea. Procedure was to start the routine all over again until it was safe to dive with no leaks and continue on our sea journey. When safely on our way underwater the “Fast Cruise” started. Inevitably there was one emergency after another with trained observers timing and setting up the emergencies. Typically you had a hydraulic burst in a compartment with a fire associated with it. Immediately the submariners moved to action and isolated and repaired hydraulics, while fighting fire with fire extinguishers. You could not bring water on board or you might sink the submarine. To remove the smoke and recycle air, the submarine had to surface or come to periscope depth and run the engines. *(at periscope depth was known as “snorting”)*

This required the induction mast raised to bring air aboard like a snorkel, and remove the air through the exhaust mast to clear out smoke. Under normal circumstances you “snorted” to charge the batteries since that was the only requirement for the diesel engines. With your batteries fully charged you were ready for more exercises which meant you left periscope depth and dived. The captain ordered “30 down keep 400 feet.” The helmsmen repeated the order while pushing stick fully forward to get a 30 degree down angle and reported depth every 10 feet. Simultaneously, other submariners watched hatches and valves to ensure no leaks. With the submarine at 400 feet it was a great time for a power failure of some type. *(perhaps a gyro failure)* Thus, the helmsman had no indication of bearing to steer hoping the submarine was still headed in the right direction. The gyro was repaired and the submarine would have to go back to periscope depth to get a “fix.” This normally meant latitude and longitude to know how far off course the submarine had gone due to gyro failure. Time to dive back down to 400 feet and level out for the next event whatever that might be. This scenario went on for the week with one problem after another for training.

Then the unthinkable happened—a real emergency in which one of the armed torpedoes had a fuel leak. This was extremely dangerous as OTTO fuel *(which was a very thick yellow fuel similar to the thickness of honey; and lethal)* could penetrate your skin. Our weapons technician donned a complete Hazmat Gear outfit and performed the clean-up and repair, with everything going into a special Hazmat bag. Upon completion of the repair, our weapons technician stripped off all of his Hazmat Gear and all of his regular clothing. These were put in a special bag that was brought to the control room as the weapons technician headed for the shower. The submarine surfaced and waited for a helicopter *(helicopter transfer at sea)* to come and take away the Hazmat Bag and have it flown to an incinerator and have it burned. This prevented anyone from dying due to the toxicity of the OTTO fuel.

It had been two days of continuous exercises and we still had three more days to go for our five day Fast Cruise. Virtually no submariner had time to rest except while waiting for the helicopter to show up. The helicopter transfer was completed and thankfully there were no complications to our weapons tech. Back to the routine of diving and starting the Fast Cruise exercises all over again. This time we started the dive and lost our hydroplanes that were stuck at 30 down. We were going down past 400 feet before the hydroplanes were put in manual in the forward and after torpedo rooms. Our submariners were pumping up the hydraulic system and maintaining the hydroplanes while leveling off around 600 feet. This had been a tremendous drain on the submariners. After the repair, the helmsman was given back control of the submarine.

As a submariner we are often asked "How deep can the submarine go?" The answer is typically "to the bottom" and I wonder if we as submariners ever really thought about that when we were at sea. I personally didn't contemplate that until joining Project Ojibwa wherein that question has been asked frequently. The answer of course is true but the reality of being at the very bottom of the ocean would most likely mean that that the submarine and its men would be lost forever.

The next order to come was to sit on the bottom at 800 feet and be ready to fire on anything that came through the area. This is what we called creating a "No Go Zone." In this scenario many American, British and Russian fleets were sunk *(unbeknownst to them)*, until the report was sent out and verified. Once again this proved that the Oberon Class submarines were the most dangerous submarines in the oceans. While doing their jobs efficiently and quietly, no-one could detect or find them, if they chose not to be found. This part of the exercise gave everyone a chance for 5 hours sleep with day five approaching.

The submariners had worked hard and fixed, repaired or isolated every problem in a timely fashion. Day five came and to the crew's surprise they had passed with flying colors. The emergency side of the "Fast Cruise" Training was now complete and "On watch" training commenced. This meant that the officers and men on watch were doing routine training in their departments and areas.

Once completed, the submarine surfaced and returned to Halifax for a well-deserved two days off. This is an interesting story of what a five day "Fast Cruise" might or might not have been like. I wonder what your thoughts are and if you believe it to be truth or fiction.

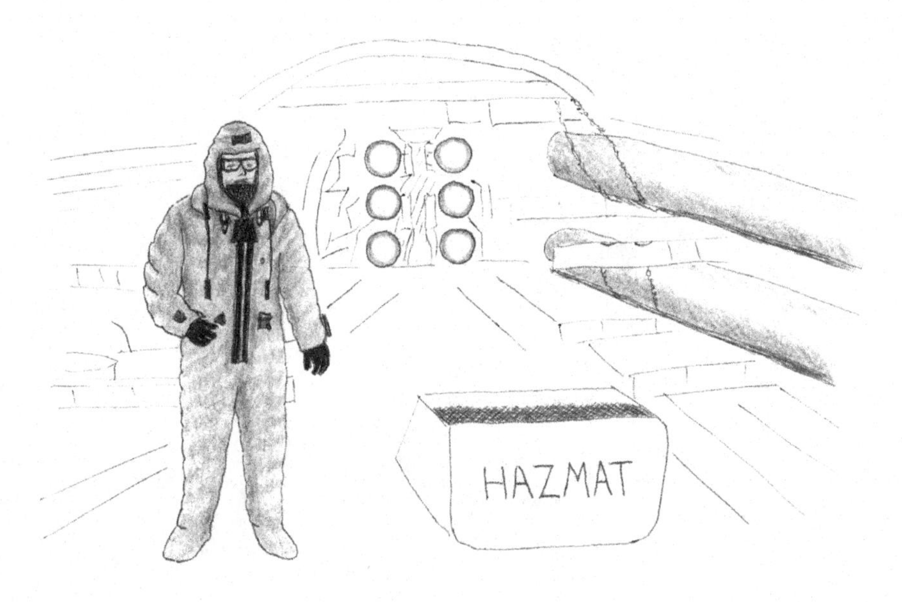

Fast Cruise

Three Canadian Submarines Operational

This is a very interesting story due to hearing that Canada never had three operational submarines. Many people in the Halifax area would see one of the submarines alongside the jetty and mention that it never left. The truth be told; it was not the same submarine at all times. It could have been HMCS (*Her Majesty's Canadian Ship*) Ojibwa one day, HMCS Onondaga the next day and HMCS Okanagan the third day and no one could tell the difference.

All three of our submarines were different inside, however outside they were the same. This kept the general public from knowing which submarine was which. During the "Cold War" one submarine came in after dark, while the one submarine that was tied to the jetty headed out to sea. This left the impression that the submarine was never moved, making it very difficult for international spies *(which were known to be in Halifax)* to steal secrets.

It is a very odd situation having all three submarines operational at the same time. The normal routine was six years operational protecting our country, followed by 3 years in refit, where systems would be upgraded and new equipment installed to give it more stealth or firepower abilities.

HMCS Ojibwa was commissioned in 1965, while HMCS Onondaga was commissioned in 1967. HMCS Okanagan arrived in 1968, just in time for HMCS Ojibwa to start its first refit. This stopped the historic event of three Canadian Submarines at sea at one time. To me this was the most likely time for this to happen but would have to wait for quite some time before it did—or did it?

From here we waited another 18 years before we would see this opportunity of three Canadian Submarines at sea at the same time. It eventually happened in the year 1986 when all three Canadian submarines were at sea for the first time in naval history. This of course would never happen again as another submarine was added to the fleet for training purposes. It was the HMS Olympus, which came after the "Cold War" was over. However they were all seen together again unfortunately alongside the jetty after decommissioning and awaiting their individual fates.

HMCS Onondaga headed to Rimouski, Quebec and was opened as a self-touring museum in 2009. It was decided that scrap was the plan until Elgin Military Museum went looking for a Military tank and was offered many tanks in the form of a submarine. HMCS Ojibwa was saved from the scrap yard and moved in November of 2012 to its present location in Port Burwell, Ontario to be part of "The Museum of Naval History."

The fate for our other Canadian Submarines was not as exciting as HMCS Onondaga's or HMCS Ojibwa's. Those two will live on forever to educate and serve as a reminder of the men from yesteryear that did amazing things to protect all Canadians and other countries from nuclear holocaust.

HMCS Okanagan and HMS Olympus were sent on their last voyage to the scrap yard and some of their secrets and adventures were potentially lost forever.

Would like to hear your thoughts and of course the ultimate question, "Is this truth or fiction?" Again there is a special page at the back of this book for you to fill out and send back. Look forward to hearing from you.

Three Canadian Submarines Operational

What's in Your Tail?

In this tale we visit our submarine preparing for weapons trials. The submarine was loading up at the Bedford Magazine. Six dummy torpedoes were loaded into the forward torpedo room for operational firings on the range. Torpedoes were loaded into the torpedo tubes while en route to the Caribbean Sea for live firings. It was decided that tubes 3 and 4 would be used on day one of firing. For day two we used 1 and 2 torpedo tubes and for day three we used tubes 5 and 6. The weapons technicians were busy ramming torpedoes into torpedo tubes for these trials. Then they hooked up the wire guiding system to operate the Mark 48 torpedoes which are still in use today.

The Submarine came into the firing range that was operated by the United States Navy and instructions were given to ensure safety of targets and safety of the submarine. For this exercise, the target was our own Destroyer Class Ship. We sat and waited for it to enter the firing range to eliminate it before it went off the range.

The option was left up to the Captain whether one or two attempts should be made. His choice was dictated by the angle on the target ship as to firing both torpedoes in one instance or to have two trials. The Captain chose two separate runs and told forward torpedo room to "open torpedo bay door 3 and prepare for firing." The coordinates for target Destroyer were confirmed by sonar operators, and the Captain on the attack periscope. The information was fed to the Fire Control System and relayed to the torpedo. The time had come for the live firing and the Captain ordered "Fire number 3 and prepare number 4 for firing." Everything went as planned and day one torpedoes from 3 and 4 were fired successfully. The destroyer was sunk on both attempts. This gave certification to tubes 3 and 4 operational and ready for action.

Day two turned out to be the same, with the exception of firing both torpedoes in sequence at our Destroyer and once again being successful at sinking her. Torpedo tubes 1 and 2 were then certified operational and ready for action.

Day three started out the same as day one planning to fire tubes 5 and 6 in two separate drills. Tube 5 was fired and again successful but after firing tube 6 things went wrong. Approximately 20 seconds after firing, the sound room went frantic "torpedo, torpedo, torpedo bearing red 145" and repeated it. The Captain on attack periscope said "What are you doing? There is nothing at that location." Sound room again reported "Torpedo, torpedo, torpedo red 155." Captain furiously said "Remove the men from the sound room." Then we heard a huge bang in the after area of the submarine on the port side. Captain looked around and said "Surface submarine to ensure no damage has been taken." We surfaced the submarine and to the Captain's embarrassment we had our torpedo stuck in the after-casing.

We took extra time heading back to Halifax and went in after dark, had the dummy torpedo removed from the casing, put duct tape over the 21 inch hole; spray painted it black and headed back to sea. We came in the next day with no outside knowledge we had been back the night before.

Wonder what ever became of that Captain as he never returned to the submarine for the next patrol? Perhaps he was promoted to a desk job but not sure of that. I am sure he would always remember that day he told the sonar room to be removed as he received the torpedo in the submarine's tail.

This is quite a story and wonder if it is true or false. At least you get to decide and any comments are appreciated as we go through different tales in this book to give you some idea of what it might have been like.

What's in Your Tail?

Riders at Sea

This tale starts with our submariners in the North Atlantic Ocean waiting to rendezvous with the HMS Hermes for Operation "Postal Run."

This operation required eight riders from the SBS *(Special Boat Service)*. These were the men that are highly trained in various military applications *(often referred as "Black Ops")* and similar to the Navy Seals of today.

Our mission as submariners was to deliver these men to the coast of an unknown country to pick up the mail or a package due to the nature of its "Top Secret" designation.

The submarine received the destination at sea to ensure that no other countries found out about this "Top Secret" mission and then headed to the Gulf of Finland and into the Baltic Sea.

In the meantime, the members of the SBS prepared their rafts and other essential equipment. This consisted of diving gear and waterproof cases for their weapons which included sniper rifles, machine guns and pistols.

They put up hammocks to sleep on in the forward torpedo room *(above the torpedoes)* and awaited their orders to disembark when the submarine was in position.

It was a 48 hour trip to the location known as Saint Petersburg, USSR at the time. The exact area was confirmed by the radioman through the crypto gear just in case there was a last minute change.

We arrived off the coast and watched, and waited for the opportunity to move in close enough to let the SBS off the submarine. If we were unable to surface, *(which was most unlikely)* the SBS men would have to exit the submarine another way. Our torpedo tubes were fully loaded so that would not have been an option this time around. We cycled them through the forward torpedo room "escape hatch" and when their black rafts were inflated and ready to go they hooked a rope up between them. The submarine maintained periscope depth and pulled them in as close as possible to shore using the attack periscope.

As we passed Kronstadt *(an island 30 kilometers to the west of St. Petersburg)* our riders went through the escape hatch and the submarine towed them as close as possible to St. Petersburg. The submarine headed back to the east of Kronstadt until ready to make pickup in three days.

We met our riders again 72 hours after they completed their mission ashore where they picked up the package. This package turned out to be from a known double-agent who was at risk of being identified by the KGB *(known as a military unit for gathering intelligence and counter intelligence)* but for the sake of this tale we will call him "Mr. X." He will be in another volume of "Submariner Tales" in much more detail.

The pick-up was successful with no casualties and once again our submarine and submariners did their duty to Queen and Country.

This tale is unique in the fact that our submarines were involved with known spies *(the real 007's)* and maintained their secrets to ensure your safety in years to come. Wondering what you think and is this tale true or false? Use the page at the back of the book and enjoy the upcoming tales.

Riders at Sea

Operation "Sneak Peak"

This tale has our submarine and submariners in the North Atlantic Ocean headed toward the Baltic Sea.

The Captain received radio intelligence that the Russian Project 1826 was completed and was headed out to sea. Our orders were to move into very close quarters and gather any and all information of this new spy ship while remaining undetected.

The submarine waited for confirmation of launch and stayed in contact with aircraft and all radio chatter from Russia waiting for Project 1826 to head our way so we could move in under her port side as she passed by.

The Captain took pictures from the Attack Periscope of this new spy ship known as Project 1826. He took pictures from about 20 feet from Project 1826's port side and turned back down her starboard side taking the photos of her underside which had noticeable sonar equipment and other underwater communications.

Upon completion of the hull photos we moved to 1000 feet away and then came in at periscope depth. There we photographed her upper side with huge communications ball masts, which was armed with deck guns and had no visible radar mast. The hull number was CCB 493 and was the first of Russia's intelligence gathering fleet.

The action helmsman was on the OMC *(one man control)* for this highly secretive mission. If anything went wrong, the danger for the submarine was that the periscope ran into Project 1826 and became like a can opener, sinking this new spy ship and ultimately taking the submarine down to the depths of the ocean, killing all aboard. The first pass down the port side from bow to stern was an incredible sight to see as it was recorded on video. Submariners in the control room were watching on the small monitor to ensure the Captain was getting everything recorded.

Project 1826 went by without knowing the Canadian submarine had taken video photos of the port underside of Russia's secret spy ship. A few hours later the submarine went down her starboard side from aft to stern getting her underside recorded. The submarine headed away and went to periscope depth to take the photos of her topside.

Thankfully nothing went wrong and we have the first known photos of the new Project 1826 spy ship. This was given to Maritime Command upon our return to Halifax to be presented to our allies.

After presentation it was decided that Project 1826 from now on would be known as a "Balzam Class" intelligence gathering spy ship with the name of "Aziya."

Another wonderful tale in which the capabilities of submarines and the submariners who worked aboard to keep their country safe from the threat of the "Cold War" is told, leaving the question "Is this truth or fiction you decide?" Feel free to let me know by filling in the pages at the back of this book.

Operation “Sneak Peak”

Close Call

This submariner story starts off as the submarine is headed out from three days shore leave in Bermuda on the way back to Halifax.

The submarine dove 100 miles north of Bermuda for routine patrol back home. Two days into our patrol the sonar operator picked up a contact to port at Red 35 true bearing 325 hearing faint cavitation *(a noise made by air bubbles from the propellers of another vessel)*. Captain wanted a classification as to whether it was hostile or friendly. Sound room reported "We have a second contact at Green 45 true bearing 045 moving fast towards us," then lost in a sound channel. Captain responded "Get me that contact again" and ordered the submarine to "ultra-quiet state" *(this is where all unnecessary equipment is turned off and submariners not on watch are to head to their bunks and remain quiet)*.

The sound room was intently searching the previous bearing plus or minus 25 degrees and had picked back up the second contact. This time it was closer and was giving off a signature. Captain asked "What have we got sound room?" Sonar operator replied "It's a hostile sir, as we have a 50 line and its propeller system is 2 X 3 *(2 shafts and 3 blades)* classification Soviet submarine Yankee class, sir." Captain wanted to know if we could get its full signature and headed to the safe to pull the Soviet submarine intelligence file. Captain returned with top secret file and gave it to the sound room operators.

Six hours later the Soviet submarine was close enough, giving off its complete signature which matched Soviet Submarine K219 carrying 16 missiles and 34 warheads. Captain ordered "Action stations remain at ultra-quiet state and I want to know what the first contact is." The submarine was now at its highest state with the best operators on all of the equipment aboard. Captain decided to turn to port and head towards first contact to get a classification.

One hour later we had the first contact back and sound room reported a turbine whine and contact was moving towards us. Sonar operator got the 60 line and reported it as a friendly submarine; likely American. Captain ordered, "I want a classification" and headed for the American file in the safe and gave it to the sound room. He wanted to know exactly which submarine this was.

Our submariners were now in between two nuclear submarines and neither one of them knew there was a Canadian Submarine in the middle. Captain asked sound room "Do you think they are playing cat and mouse with each other or are they both on patrol in the same zone?"

Sound room stated, "Based on our projected ranges for each submarine, they are playing cat and mouse and we are right in the middle of the two of them." Captain asked, "Have you got the classification for our friendly American submarine?"

Sonar operator, "Yes sir it is a Los Angeles Class Fast Attack Submarine and so far we don't have her complete signature." Captain then said, "It looks like we will be at action stations for the next few hours so let me know when you have the name of our American sub." A short while later sound room passed information out that the American submarine was USS Augusta (SSN 710) carrying Tomahawk, Harpoon Missiles, and the same Mark 48 torpedoes that our submarine carried.

Sonar reported "They have just crisscrossed our bow and stern and now are closer and potentially dangerous to us." Captain reported "We now have K219 on our port side headed towards USS Augusta which is now on our starboard side." K219 is now the cat and USS Augusta is the mouse with us still stuck in the middle. Sound room replies "K219 is headed right at us sir." Captain said "30 down, *(helmsman pushed the one man control stick fully down to follow this order)* take us to 700 feet" to get out of K219's way.

This turned out to be a move that saved the submarine from being sunk as K219 hit the port side of our submarine and continued on her course. Captain yelled out "Damage report!" To our surprise everything was intact and we had no noticeable damage. The submarine slowly moved from 700 feet to periscope depth so that we could charge the batteries and send out divers to assess any hull damage in a safe zone 400 miles away.

Divers returned with their report. "We have been hit port side amidships with no penetration through ballast tanks." We are safe and await radio orders to return to Halifax or remain in area 800 miles north of Bermuda. We received radio transmission to head to Florida and enjoy a few days while Maritime Command decided our next move.

We have finished another tale and await your thoughts and comments on whether this is truth or fiction. Hope you enjoyed another adventure of submarines and submariners during the "Cold War."

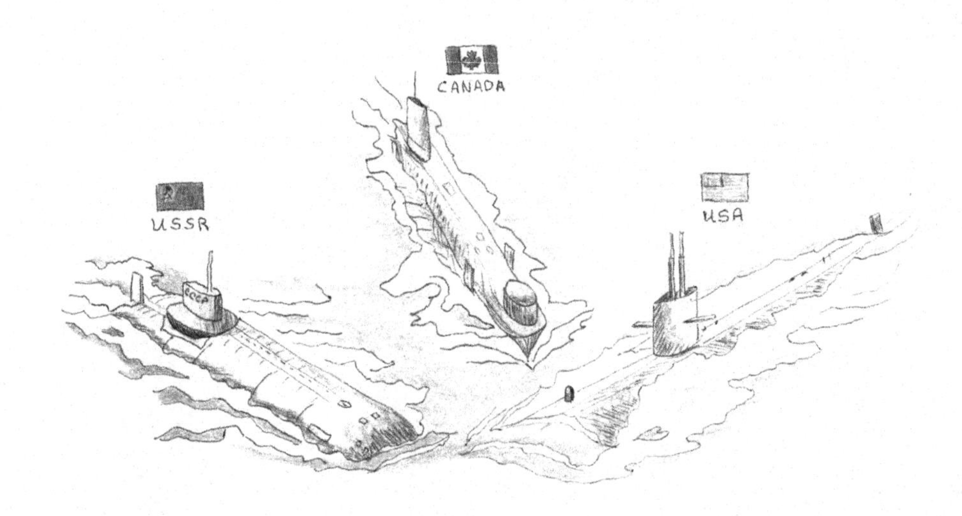

Margaret Kipp
2013

Close Call

Acknowledgements

Cover Art and Illustrations Special thanks to Margaret Kipp for doing an incredible job of creating the cover as well as all other illustrations for "Submariner Tales."

Margaret is a well-known artist with works in many galleries and studios and has done paintings for the Presidents of the United States of America.

Editor: Randall Pierce from Arkansas, USA

Publisher: The excellent team that was put together to assemble this book by AuthorHouse.

Life of a Submariner: Special thanks to Melissa Schneider who wrote an article for the St. Thomas/Elgin Weekly News.

Notable persons that assisted with the making of this book:

To my beautiful wife Lynda Lewis, who proof read all pages and gave support to the completion of this book in a timely manner.

To The Elgin Military Museum who gave the opportunity to write this book and assisted with legal and financing costs to get the tales out to the public.

To Payne Kipp who donated to The Elgin Military Museum on behalf of this project for initial printing.

To the volunteers aboard HMCS Ojibwa during the restoration; for public tours who enjoyed listening to my tales, and wanted more for the public and themselves to understand Submariners and the "Cold War."

To LGT Family Church who assisted me on my Spiritual Journey and the Men's Bible Study that inspired me with the first tale in this book.

Truth or Fiction You Decide

Tale 1: The First Submarine and Submariner Known to Man

I believe this to be: Truth _______ Fiction_______

Comments:

Tale 2: Canadian Submarine in the Falklands

I believe this to be: Truth _______ Fiction_______

Comments:

Tale 3: No More Volunteers for Silent Service

I believe this to be: Truth _______ Fiction_______

Comments:

Tale 4: Submariners Ashore

I believe this to be: Truth _______ Fiction_______

Comments:

Tale 5: Fast Cruise

I believe this to be: Truth _______ Fiction_______

Comments:

Tale 6: Three Canadian Submarines Operational

I believe this to be: Truth _______ Fiction_______

Comments:

Tale 7: What's In Your Tail?

I believe this to be: Truth _______ Fiction_______

Comments:

Tale 8: Riders at Sea

I believe this to be: Truth _______ Fiction_______

Comments:

Tale 9: Operation Sneak Peak

I believe this to be: Truth _______ Fiction_______

Comments:

Tale 10: Close Call

I believe this to be: Truth _______ Fiction_______

Comments:

Send to: Dean S. Lewis, C/O The Museum of Naval History,

3 Pitt Street, PO Box 250, Port Burwell, Ontario, NOJ 1T0

Donation Enclosed_______________ Receipt—Yes___ No___

Make Donations Payable to The Elgin Military Museum

OR

Send to: Kingdom Restorers, C/O LGT Family Church,

288 Commissioners Rd West, London, Ontario, N6J 1Y3

Donation Enclosed_______________ Receipt—Yes___ No___

Make Donations Payable to LGT Family Church

100 percent of all Donations go to your choice of above addresses

About the Author

Dean Scott Lewis was born in Woodstock, Ontario, Canada in 1964 and in 1972 was legally adopted by his step-father. In 1972 he changed his name to Dean Scott Roth. In March of 1982 at the age of 17 he joined the Canadian Armed Force. He was signed in by his parents while pledging allegiance to the Queen and Country at Centennial Hall in London, Ontario. He was sent to Cornwallis, Nova Scotia for "boot camp" as the last naval platoon 8214 before closing of this base.

He then headed to Halifax, Nova Scotia to be trained as a sonar operator. While on sonar course he received a posting to HMCS Annapolis which had run aground off of Halifax, tearing off their active sonar. Submariners came and asked for volunteers for submarines and as top student for his course Dean accepted. He desired to do his role as a sonar man in the Secret Service also known as the Silent Service during the "Cold War" and protect Canada.

He passed his submarine training in 1983 and received his "Dolphins" and became one of the most highly trained members of the Canadian Armed Forces, like his qualified brothers aboard submarines. Some of his duties included Action Stations Helmsman *(potentially the hardest position onboard submarines, especially when snorting)*, Bar Manager onboard and inboard at the Jolly Roger Mess, and he became one of the top 10 sonar operators of that time period. He served on board all three submarines—Ojibwa, Okanagan and Onondaga in his six and a half years, receiving an Honorable Discharge in 1988.

In 2008 Dean and his wife Lynda with a friend Nora started Kingdom Restorers when they were told Joyce Meyer Ministries would be closing its Canadian office to help anyone with addictions. Dean was diagnosed an alcoholic in the 1998 and GOD removed that addiction in 2005 when Dean found a new reason to live as a born again Christian.

Kingdom Restorers mission statement is simply "Restoring GODS Kingdom One Opportunity at a Time". You can help by filling out the Truth or Fiction section and returning it with a donation. 100 % of the funding will go to helping others with this mission. Thank You in advance.

Dean and Lynda attend LGT Family Church and would be honored to meet you there. LGT Family Church's Vision Statement follows.

Zechariah 4:6

'Not by might nor by power, but by my Spirit,' says the LORD ALMIGHTY.

—loving GOD demonstrated in lives of holiness, set in prayer and obedience to the Scriptures

—loving each person within LGT by living in unity and caring for one another

—the Evangelistic call to reach our diverse community and the world

—inspired preaching and worship expression

—group ministries where believers grow from spiritual infancy to children, young men & women, to spiritual reproducing fathers & mothers

—spiritual gifts released by GOD and exercised in our lives

—caring for the spiritually and physically needy

Dean presently lives in St. Thomas, Ontario with his beautiful wife Lynda and they have 5 beautiful daughters and three wonderful grandchildren. Dean is presently working, on the restoration of HMCS Ojibwa in Port Burwell, with great volunteers to get HMCS Ojibwa open to the public for July 1, 2013. Dean thanks GOD, Lynda, family and friends for the support in making "Submariner Tales, Truth or Fiction You Decide" possible.

Hope to see you at the Museum of Naval History so you can enjoy this incredible artifact. "Cold War Submarine Ojibwa"